WHERE IS MY HOME?

Based on a true story

JOAN ROMNEY GROVES

"Danny!" shouted Brooke.
"Tally has four baby kittens!"

"Look, their eyes are closed," Danny said.

"Mom said we shouldn't touch the kittens or mother cat will move them," Brooke cautioned.

Every morning, the children checked on the kittens. Soon, the kittens opened their eyes and crawled around the garage. The Jakes family named them: Shadow, Tiger, Timberwolf and Sonic.

Brooke and Danny played, teased, and entertained the kittens. The kittens loved the attention -- all BUT SONIC. Sonic always hissed and ran away.

Danny had scratches from holding him.

"Sonic is mean," he sobbed to his mother.

"I'm sorry," she said comforting him. "He seems to have a wild streak."

When the kittens were two months old, they were ready to leave their mother. Mrs. Jakes said, "Five cats are too many for our family. We must find homes for them."

A neighbor, Mrs. Hammond, selected Shadow immediately.

Danny's best friend, Alex, and his family adopted Tiger.

Two kittens were left when Mrs. Newbold
brought her children to choose a pet.
Sonic growled and refused to be touched.
Timberwolf purred.

"We'll take Timberwolf," they agreed.

"That's fine," said Mrs. Jakes, "but we still need a home for Sonic. Do you know anyone who will take him?"

Mrs. Newbold shook her head.

"I'm afraid we won't be able to find a home for him. He is not like the other cats. He is mean to the kids. I think he was born to be wild."

"My mom has a barn near a creek where some wild cats live," said Mrs. Newbold. "Sonic could live there. He would have food, water, shelter and open fields to roam."

"He would probably like that," Mrs. Jakes replied.

The next day Mrs. Newbold struggled to get Sonic into a box. Once she did, she drove him 30 miles to his new home in South Jordan. Anxious to get out, Sonic scratched a small hole in the box. When the lid was opened, he dashed into the field.

Sonic was excited about his new surroundings. He sniffed the young alfalfa, listened to the babbling creek and felt the warm sun on his back. Butterflies and moths danced overhead.

He teetered on fences, climbed tall trees, and frolicked in the open fields. He attacked toads, field mice, and garter snakes.

Sonic loved his freedom. He had no rules to follow and no one to please but himself.

Hooray! A new home! he thought as he spied an old building nearby.

As he entered the barn, the resident cats hissed and growled at him. When he curled up to sleep, a grey cat attacked him.

I cannot live here, he decided. *Where is my home?*

Sonic moved on looking for a home and friends. As he climbed over a pile of rocks, a weasel beckoned him closer. Slowly, Sonic crept forward when fear filled his body. *This is a trap,* he thought. He whirled around, lunged across the field and crawled under a barbed-wire fence. The weasel nipped at his tail.

Feeling hungry, Sonic spied a mother killdeer dragging a broken wing. As he crept closer, she chattered, "Kee-dee, kee-dee," and flew away.

Another trick, thought Sonic.

A black and white animal waddled toward him. Sonic thought, *Now I have a friend.*

But his playmate turned his back, stomped his feet, raised his tail and sprayed him. Sonic stunk for days.

Later, Sonic spied two trout on the river bank. *My lucky day,* he thought, as he began nibbling on a fishtail. Suddenly, a swift kick sent him sailing into the icy water. A teenage boy yelled, "Get away from my fish, you lousy cat!"

Fighting for his life, Sonic pulled himself out of the river. He was cold and wet. As he shook the water from his fur, he thought, *Where is my home?*

Shorter days and longer nights chilled the air. To keep warm, Sonic nestled in a bed of leaves. As he drifted off to sleep, he felt a breeze ruffle his fur. He opened his eyes to see a large owl swooping toward him. "Hoot! Hoot!" screeched the owl. Trembling, Sonic raced into the darkness. Coyotes howled in the distance.

That night, Sonic curled up in a hollow log. The trunk was rough, unlike the soft fur of his mother. *Where is my home?* he wondered.

As Sonic passed a nearby elementary school, he heard children laughing and playing. He followed a boy home where Sonic gobbled a leftover tuna fish sandwich.

"Mom, can we keep this cat? He likes me," said the boy.

"We'll see," she said.

The next morning, Sonic was gone.

Sonic came to a city street. The traffic was crowded and dangerous. With lightning speed, he darted between cars. Brakes screeched and horns honked as he splashed through rain puddles. Thunder rattled the air.

"Yeoow!" he shrieked shivering with fright. *Where is my home?*

Garbage cans became Sonic's source of food. As he scavenged through scraps of pizza, salad greens and French fries, the garbage can fell over and crashed. Dogs barked and chased him. "GRRUUFFF!" snarled a pit bull in his face.

Sonic sprang up a tree and stayed until the dog backed away.

Sonic realized the world can be dangerous. He became unhappy, scared and lonely. *I cannot stay here*, he said to himself. *Where is my home?*

To calm his fears, he sipped water from a still pond and then wandered over the green hills. A kind deer licked his head as if to soothe his broken heart. *I have no home,* thought Sonic.

Temperatures dropped to freezing as Sonic trudged on. Swirling snowflakes fell from the sky.

The cold, wet winter months were long. Red, green and gold lights flickered in the city and beautiful music filled the air.

In the park, a display of people and animals admiring a baby drew his attention. A bright star beamed down on the scene. Heavenly peace filled the air. His spirit was uplifted.

Spring's longer, warmer days brought a welcome relief. Tulips and daffodils embraced the sun.

Farmers planted new crops. Sonic enjoyed nibbling the young plants. Sometimes the chemicals on the plants gave him a tummy ache.

Months passed when Sonic reached Orem City. He had traveled through seven towns. Sleeping was tough. Finding food was even harder. Sonic longed for a home.

As the sun peeked over the horizon, Sonic spied a red-brick house with white shutters. Familiar smells of lilacs and sweaty sneakers filled the air. He wandered into an open garage and snuggled into a worn-out quilt. *Can this be my home?* he wondered as he fell asleep.

Two hours later, Danny opened the door to a surprise. He shouted, "Mom! Mom! Sonic is back!" He swooped him into his arms. Sonic purred contentedly.

"That's impossible!" exclaimed Mother. "Sonic would never let you pick him up. Besides, he has been gone for nine months."

Brooke rushed in and hugged Sonic. "Meow," he said, greeting her. "Mom, it is him!" exclaimed Brooke. "He likes us now. Can we keep him?"

"This is amazing!" Mother replied. "He had to walk 30 miles to get here. Of course , we'll keep him. This is his home! He knows it and we know it!"

As Sonic went to sleep that night, his last thoughts were: I am home! HOME AT LAST!